J.otto Seibold has written, cowritten, and illustrated many children's books, including *Olive, the Other Reindeer*. He was also the first person to draw children's books on a computer. With *Other Goose*, J.otto introduces a new element to his art—spray-painted backgrounds (which have given him very colorful fingernails). J.otto lives in Oakland, California.

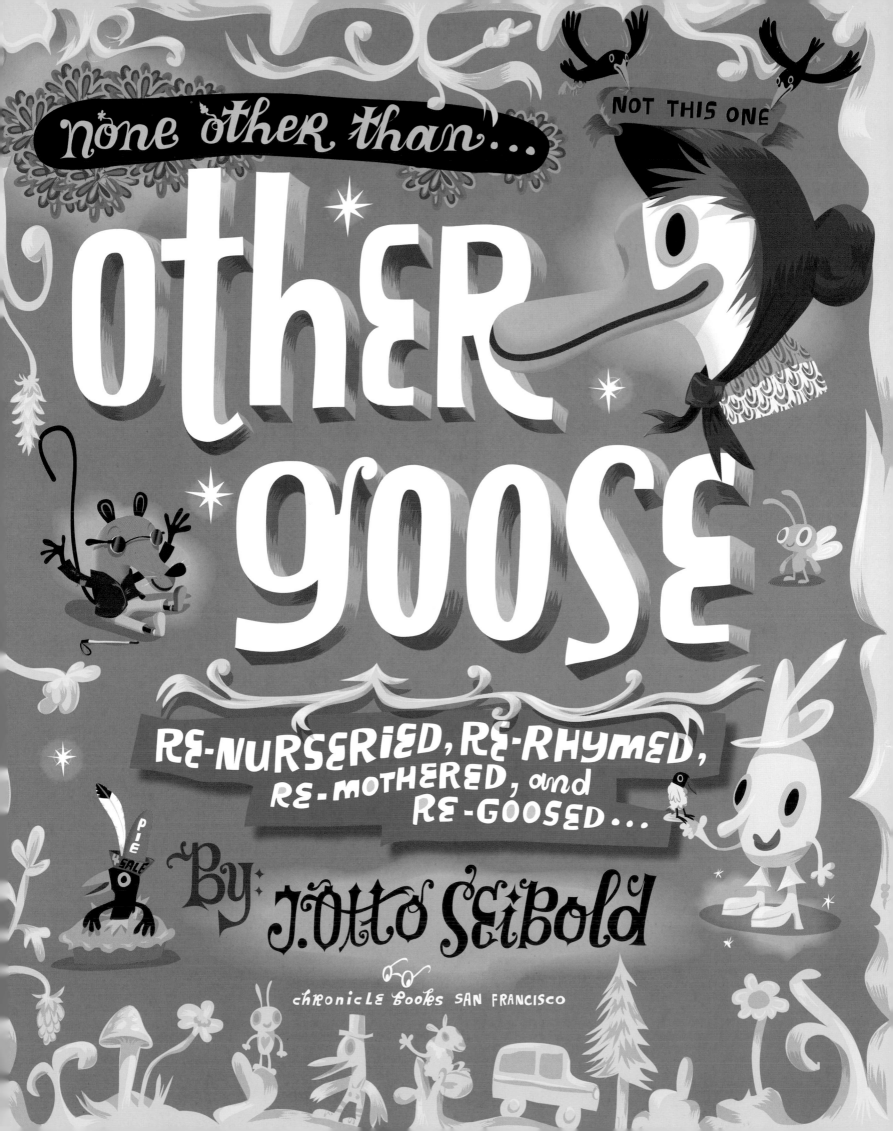

none other than...

NOT THIS ONE

OtheR goose

RE-NURSERIED, RE-RHYMED, RE-MOTHERED, and RE-GOOSED...

BY J. OttO SEibold

PIE SALE

CHRONICLE BOOKS SAN FRANCISCO

Love always to T. A. and U.   –J.o.S.

SPECIAL THANK YOU
to ANDREA MENOTTI
FOR ALL HER HARD WORK
AND BRIGHT IDEAS!

Library of Congress Cataloging-in-Publication Data available.
ISBN 978-0-8118-6882-2

Book design by J.otto Seibold, Amelia Anderson, and Eloise Leigh.
Typeset in Other Goose by J.otto Seibold.
The illustrations in this book were composed on a computer and with
spray paint on wood panels with generous help from Amelia Walsh.

AND GRATITUDE TO
PIEDMONT DENTAL by DESIGN
thanks FOR THE GOLD TEETH!!

Manufactured by C&C Offset, Longgang, Shenzhen, China,
in June 2010.

10 9 8 7 6 5 4 3 2 1

This product conforms to CPSIA 2008.

Chronicle Books LLC
680 Second Street, San Francisco, California 94107

www.chroniclekids.com

this Book
BELONGS
→ to ↘

your name

3
bag of wool

TICKET

2
6
5

CONTENTS

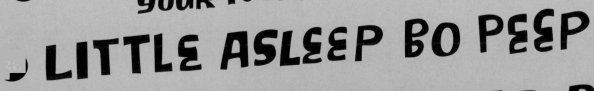

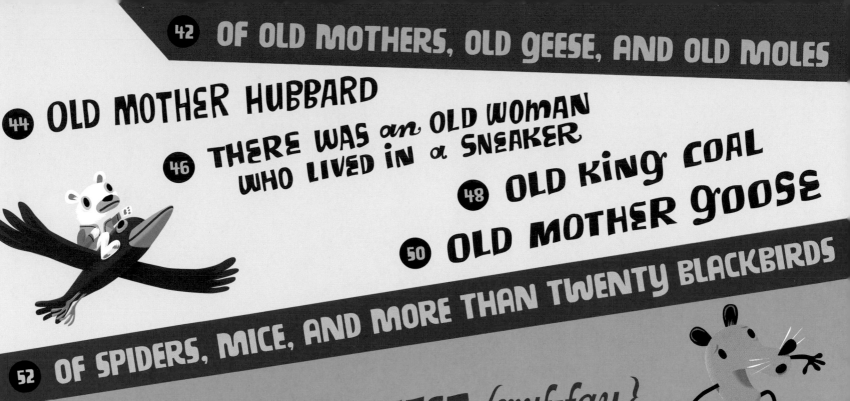

AN INTRODUCTION FROM OTHER GOOSE

Let it be said that it is difficult for me to gather my thoughts in any other form than rhyme. But as this volume of altered classics may be shelved among "Mother Goose" books, a few words of explanation may be in order.

First, let me tell you a little secret about Mother Goose. SHE IS NOT A GOOSE! She is actually a person. And while I certainly compliment her rhymes, some of them have grown quite dusty over time. I mean, what good is a pocket full of rye anymore, I ask you?

That is why I am here.

I am actually a goose.

And I know how to rhyme.

I have taken Mother Goose's rhymes and, let us say, re-nurseried them. I have made them more modern, more fresh, and well . . . more Goosian. I have also found an illustrator named J.otto Seibold (who is not a goose) to create pictures for my rhymes. I find a rhyme is rather lonely without a picture.

Rhymes are important, you see. Before there were books, important thoughts were passed down by way of rhyme. Why rhymes? Because they get stuck in your head! That's just how rhymes are. Especially Goosian rhymes. They are Extremely Memorable Words.

So, without further ado, I present my collection, recorded as I remember them best: the Other Goose book of nursery rhymes.

— Other Goose

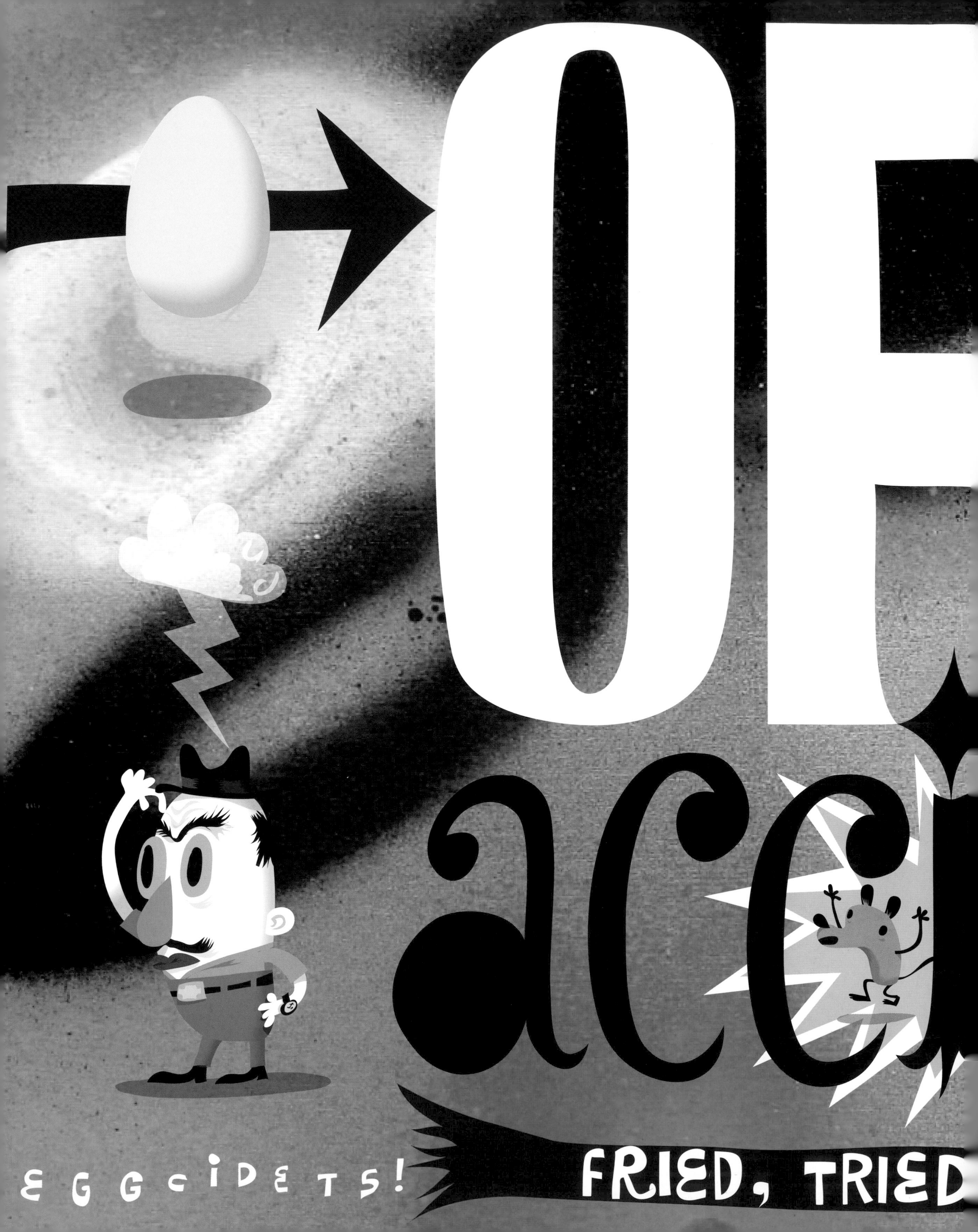
OF
acc
EGGCIDETS!
FRIED, TRIED

Eggs

and

Tents

and JUSTIFIED!!!

PART ONE

Humpty Dumpty wasn't that tall.
Humpty Dumpty went to the mall.
He searched all the shelves
again and again
until Humpty found
a true bargain.

PART TWO

Humpty Dumpty went for a stroll.
Humpty Dumpty stepped in a hole.
His shoe got stuck;
he was in a bind.
So Humpty had to leave
that shoe behind.

PART THREE

Humpty Dumpty had a big shoe.
Humpty Dumpty used to have two.
He clopped in a circle
again and again,
but his shoes would never
be together again.

EPILOGUE

Three Days Later. . .
All the park's squirrels
and all the store's mice
turned Humpty's shoe
into something not nice.

JACK and JILL (and BILL)

Jack and Jill
and a pickle named Bill
strolled atop a mountain.
Jack bent down
to pick some dill,
and the pickle jumped in
the fountain.

JACK B. NIMBLE

Jack B. Nimble,
the name did stick.
Over the candle,
over the wick,
Jack be famous
for this trick.

Jack B. Nimble

THE SPLATS

Jack Splat paints abstract.
His wife paints country scenes.
Together they fill the canvas up
and live the life serene.

PETER PUMPKIN PICKLE PEPPER

Peter Pumpkin Pickle Pepper
played the pipe—
no clarineter!
Played in storms,
any weather!
Played because it made him better.

SIMPLE SIMON

Simple Simon was good at rhyming
and not a whole lot else.

He went to the fair
for that is where
he went to fetch his pie.

But up in his head,
his thoughts instead
began to churn and fly.

So just as before,
he came back to his door
forgetting what it was he went for.

That's Jack Horner
over in the corner.
He doesn't get a poem!

LITTLE BOY BLUE COME BLOW YOUR TUBA!

Little boy blue
come blow your tuba.
The sheep are in Venice,
and the cow's in Aruba.
But where is the boy
in charge of them all?
He's chasing chickens in Nepal.
Time to worry?
Not at all!
Here's his number . . .
Give him a call!

LITTLE ASLEEP BO PEEP

Little Bo Peep
did fail to keep
her little lambs beside her.
She went to sleep
while counting sheep,
and the lambs went far and wider.

Some climbed trees,
some chased bees,
and one even flew on a glider.

Back they crept
while Bo still slept
and hatched a plan to hide there.

When she woke,
no lamb spoke.
In fact, they all got quieter.

She searched and called
and almost bawled.
Then they all jumped out and surprised her!

MARY HAD A LITTLE BAND

Mary had a singing lamb
whose voice was widely known.
Everywhere the lamb would sing,
he never sang alone.
Mary played a guitar jam
with her little lamb.
And so they played throughout the years
and all throughout the land.

BLAH BLAH BLACK SHEEP

Baa baa black sheep,
have you any wool?
"Hmmm, let me see,"
he said after a lull.
"This is for the master;
this is for the dame;
this is for someone
who lives down the lane...
so, no!"

OF OLD MOTHERS, OLD

and OLD

OLD MOTHER HUBBARD

Old Mother Hubbard
thought she had it covered,
and her dog had thought that, too.
Then she went to the cupboard
where she discovered . . .
No bones! No food! Boo-hoo!

THERE WAS an OLD WOMAN WHO LIVED IN a SNEAKER

There was an old woman
who lived in a sneaker.
She had a great big stereo speaker.
She played it so loud,
her hearing grew weaker.
Tell me,
could this story get any bleaker?

OLD KING COAL

Old King Coal
was a dreary old mole,
and that was all he could be.
He called on the phone,
for he was alone,
"Come fiddlers, play music for me."
The fiddlers did fiddle
and fiddled for a fee:
Three songs for three ninety-three!

OLD MOTHER GOOSE

Old Mother Goose
(who wasn't a goose)
jumped up on a gander.
But after a while,
the gander thought
it might be best to land 'er.

OF SPIDERS, MICE AND MORE THAN TWENTY BLACKBIRDS

LITTLE MISS MUFFET *{muf-fay}*

Little Miss Muffet
held an insect buffet
featuring curds and whey.
Along came a spider
with a jug of cherry cider
who said,
"I think I'll join you today."

HICKORY DICKORY CLOCK

Hickory dickory clock,
the mice ran up in a flock.
The clock struck one;
the rest had fun.
Hickory dickory clock.

DON'T SING A SONG of SIXPENCE

Why sing a song of sixpence?
That money doesn't make sense.
And who puts blackbirds in a pie?
I really have to wonder why.

Four and twenty blackbirds, too.
That's more than just a few.
I'd say it's quite a large amount,
but it's up to you to count.

And is a pocket
a good place to keep rye?
I'd ask the king,
but he's been poked
in his royal eye!

HEY DIDDLE FIDDLE

Hey diddle diddle,
there's a cat and a fiddle.
The concert's inside at noon.
At a part in the middle,
the cat cried a little,
and the plate left early with the spoon.
The little doggie clapped,
the toothpaste stayed capped,
and the cow cheered along with the moon.

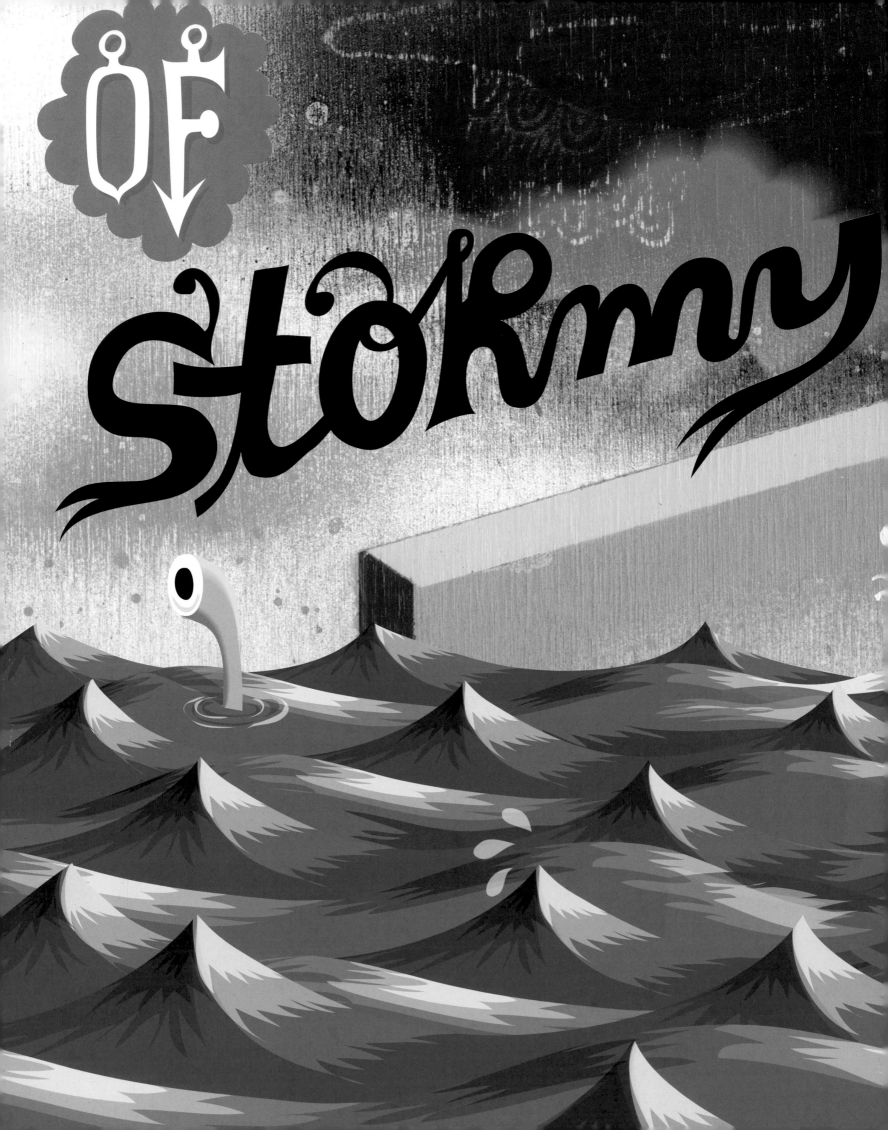

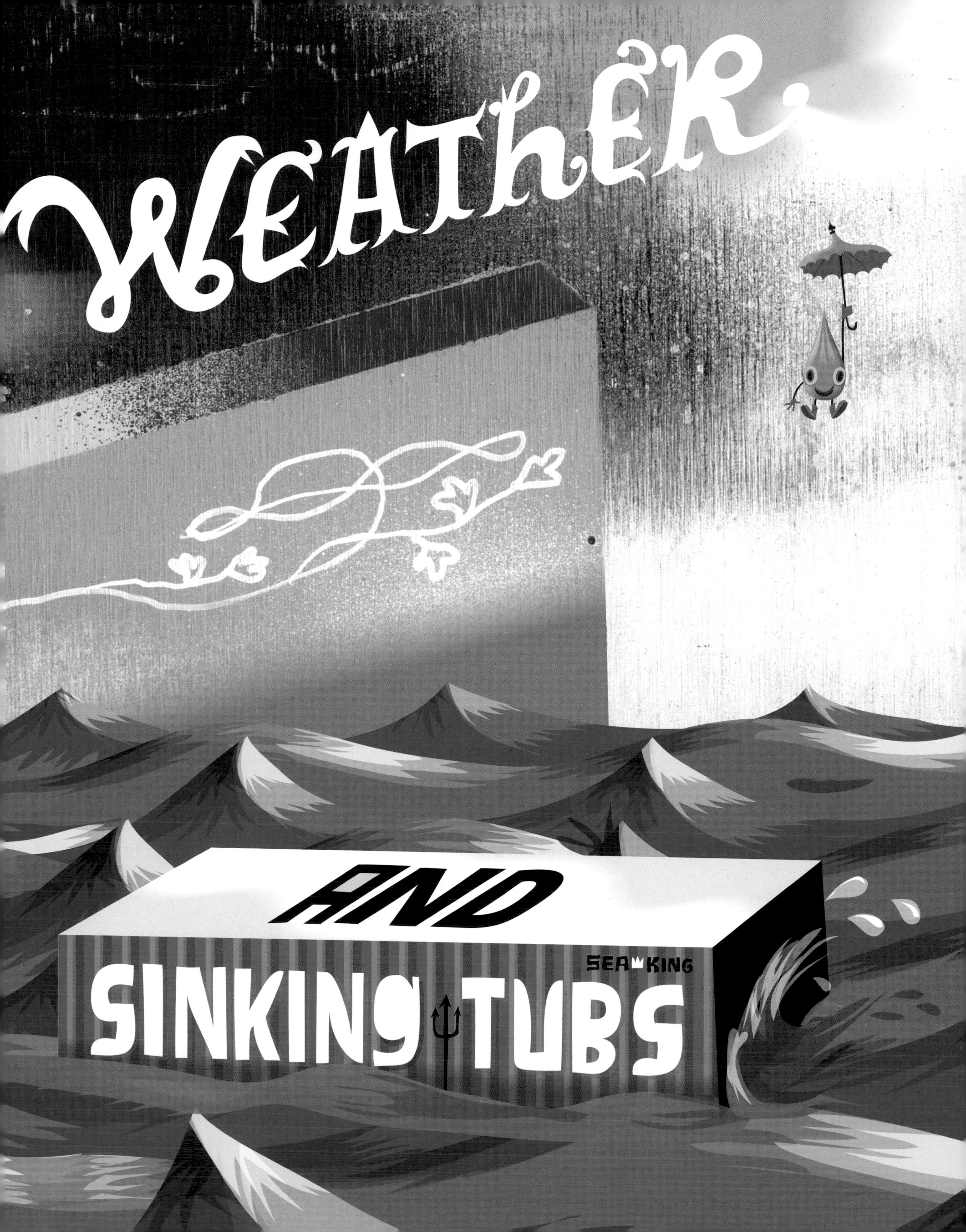
WEATHER
AND
SINKING TUBS
SEA KING

RAIN, RAIN, DON'T GO AWAY

Rain, rain,
don't go away.
The sun can shine
some other day.

RUB-A-DUB-DUB ⚓

Rub-a-dub-dub
three guys in a tub,
sailing to who-knows-where.

Blub-a-blub-blub
there's a hole in the tub,
causing quite a scare.

Glub-a-glub-glub
three birds in a sub;
the tub they did repair!

IT'S RAINING, IT'S BORING!

It's raining, it's boring.
The snoring creaks the flooring.
With that said,
go to bed,
and I'll see you in the morning!

THIRTEEN
FOURTEEN
grunting
SNORTING
FIFTEEN
SIXTEEN
Spider
SEVENTEEN
Eighteen
SHEEP